Benedict Kiely has come to be regarded as one of Ireland's finest literary writers. Born near Dromore, in County Tyrone in 1919 his long and successful career spans the writing of novels, short stories and memoirs. He is well known as a raconteur and broadcaster on TV and radio.

His adult novels include *The Cards of the Gambler*, *The Captain and the Whiskers*, *Honey Seems Bitter* and *Dogs Enjoy the Morning* among many other works. *The Trout in the Turnhole* is his first children's book.

ABOUT THE ILLUSTRATOR

Niamh Sharkey is an exciting new young Irish illustrator. Her colour work has appeared on several children's book covers. This is her first book for Wolfhound Press. Niamh lives and works in Sandymount in Dublin.

The Trout
in the
Turnhole

*Dedicated to all readers who are young and hopeful enough to
believe that any fisherman could ever catch
The Old One.*

The Trout
in the
Turnhole

Benedict Kiely

PETER, son of Jamesy the milkman.

Illustrated by Niamh Sharkey

WOLFHOUND PRESS

First published 1995 by
WOLFHOUND PRESS Ltd
68 Mountjoy Square
Dublin 1

Wolfhound Press receives financial assistance from the Arts Council/ An Chomhairle Ealaíon, Dublin.

British Library Cataloguing in Publication Data
A catalogue record for this book is available from the British Library

ISBN 0-86327-451-X

Cover illustration: Niamh Sharkey
Cover design: Joe Gervin
Typesetting: Wolfhound Press
Printed in the UK by Cox & Wyman Ltd., Reading, Berks.

1

Peter was the son of Jamesy, the milkman, and of Mary who was the wife of Jamesy. He was a big, strong, witless boy. He had no head for books. He had hard hands and good muscles, but no will in the world for work. His heart, though, was kind and good.

The house of Jamesy, the milkman, stood, as the house of every good milkman should stand, outside the town where the fields were green and plentiful and the cattle had room to graze. It was a small house, very clean on the outside and very tidy on the inside. For, although Jamesy and his wife had not much money they could make a little go a long way.

The walls of the house were fresh and shining with new whitewash. Great sprawling creepers spread green leaves around the windows and the doors. Here and there a red rose bloomed. The roof was thatched with straw that had the colour of bright gold. Before the house was a small garden,

radiant and perfumed with all sorts of
flowers. Behind the house there was a
large garden crowded with cabbages and
beans and potatoes. On one side of the house
was the stack of black turf, the house for the hens
and the stable for the pony. On the other side of the
house was the long byre where, in the evening, six
brown cows mooed and chewed and rattled their
headchains and waited for the milking.

In the warm evenings Peter would milk the six
brown cows until his strong fingers were cramped
with squeezing the white milk from the udder to
the shining can. In the cold mornings he yoked the
little black pony into the little blue cart. His father
helped him to lift the two large containers of milk
onto the cart. Then Peter drove off down the road
to the town, listening to the jingle of the containers
in the cart, bringing milk to the houses of people
who had neither cows nor green fields nor gardens,
and, sometimes, even to the houses of rich men

who were too lazy to milk their own cows.

With his whole heart Peter hated the business of selling milk for money to the people in the town. For not only was he a lazy fellow but he loved the dreams that he dreamed all by himself when he was as wide awake as you or me. He disliked being poor. Always in his favourite dream he made

himself a rich man, then married himself to the daughter of a king and lived in a palace forever and ever. All this went on in his mind when he sat on the cart between the lazy little pony and the two jingling, splashing containers.

He had a great fancy for the daughters of kings, although never once in his life, not even at a hiring-fair, had he laid eyes on one. Kate was only the daughter of a poor farmer and she would have been very sorrowful had she known how often Peter walked in his dreams with the daughters of kings.

When Kate dreamed, and that was only while she was asleep, she never saw a king's son. She saw only Peter who meant more to her than kings and queens and living in palaces.

One day in early June, at the time of the year when the grass in the meadows is very deep and glossy but still quite green, and when the sun is warm and the wind from the South, Peter rose in the early dawn. He and his father sat down together and ate their breakfasts. Then Peter harnessed the pony, his father helped him to lift the two containers onto the cart and he drove off towards the town.

As he went, the white, morning mists were broken over the meadows. The sun came up in the sky. The road was very dusty and very warm, and the fields beyond the hedges were green and cool and fresh.

As he sat on the cart he had a dream, a lazy dream with no palaces in it, nor princesses, but with the green grass of Creevan meadow and the Camowen river asleep in deep pools or flowing noisily over stony shallows.

He saw as clearly as if it were before his eyes the old sycamore tree, where he had hidden his rod and line and little pointed hook, and where he had a tin box filled with wriggling worms that he kept in clay and fed on milk, and on pieces of red brick crushed to a fine soft powder. He saw the pools where the trout lay. He remembered that the fish were very hungry for wriggling worms that had been fed on red brick, powdered very finely, and on milk. He dreamed of the surprise on the face of a speckled trout, discovering inside the red, wriggling worm a little pointed hook.

Then he gave his shoulders a shake and woke up properly. He was still sitting on the hard cart. The sun was very warm. He was choking with the fine dust rising, as the wheels turned and the hooves rose and fell, from the dry hot road.

So instead of following the road to the town Peter turned the pony's head into a green level of grazing land where many sheep and cattle were feeding. He crossed the smooth grass, leading the pony, until he came to a deep dyke overgrown with bushes and wild nettles. In a cool shadowy place beside a little stream he hid the two cans of milk and, when he had unharnessed and spancelled the pony, he slapped him sharply and sent him hobbling off across the rich grass.

Turning on his heel, he went alone and free

across the fields, leaping dykes and climbing stiles and ditches, bursting through hedgerows, throwing small pieces of stick at the birds, not so as to hit them but just for fun and companionship and to let them know that he was there and as happy as they were. He crossed a bog where men were working at the turf. No man spoke to him so he didn't offer to speak. When he had gone on some distance he turned his head quickly and looked back. But he didn't catch one of the working men looking after him or pointing after him. He thought that strange for men working in a bog on a warm day.

He went up out of the bog along a winding goat-track. He crossed a ridge of high land and saw before him the soft sweep of Creevan meadow and the shining water of the Camowen.

In no time at all he found the old sycamore tree where, tied closely to a long overhanging branch, he kept his rod and line and little pointed hook, and where, hidden under a flat stone, he kept his little tin box filled with red, wriggling worms. He took the rod in his right hand.

He put the tin box into his pocket and, still holding the switch that he had carried to beat the pony, he walked on to the river bank.

First of all he fished at the lower ends of the meadow where the river fell into a narrow black hole. The day was warm and he was very drowsy. So in that place he lost seven worms but caught never a fish.

Then weary of losing worms, he moved slowly towards the upper end of the meadow where the river widened out into a glistening pool and the water went whirling around and around. Tall trees on the far bank leaned out over the water. Some low branches even touched the surface. A few leaves fell now and again from those low branches and went around, like little boats that had lost their way, with the spinning water.

He put another worm on the hook and threw out the line.

'That's a poor cast,' he said. 'I'll put it out again.'

He made to pull it out. As he did so he felt the line tighten, and saw the rod bend, and saw the white flash down deep in the water. He pulled, gently at first and then with more force. The trout leaped in the air, splashed on the water and again went under.

'My joy,' shouted Peter. 'But it is a big one.'

The men in the bog might have heard him if they

had been listening.

It was a big one. It turned and twisted. It rose and sank. It leaped into the air and fell into the water. It went here and there and up and down. It pulled yards of thin line off the little spinning reel. It tried to reach the bottom and tangle the line around the friendly stones. But the hook held and the line held and the rod bent but did not break.

At last Peter drew the fish into the shallow water. Then with a turn of his wrist he threw it onto the grass of the meadow.

But as he did so the line snapped near the hook and the trout went farther than Peter had ever intended. He dropped the rod and ran after the fish. The rod fell into the river and went drifting away with the current.

Peter listened for the slither in the grass. He heard it and ran towards it, and the slither went before him as fast as the run of a rabbit. Never before had he heard of a trout that could run on the land as well as swim in the water; and from old bearded fishermen, who sat all day by the arches of stone bridges, he had heard many stories of many trout.

He saw in the grass the trail of loose line that had broken off with the hook, and very firmly he placed his foot on it. Then a voice spoke to him out of the grass.

'PETER, son of Jamesy the milkman.'

'Peter, the son of Jamesy the milkman,' said the voice.

'True for you,' said Peter. 'And who might you be?'

'I am the Trout of the Turnhole of Creevan,' said the voice. 'I am the King of All Trout and wiser than any salmon. The green pike are afraid of me. My other name is the Old One.'

'I know you now,' said Peter, and indeed he did.

All fishermen of the trout know the Old One. They have all hooked him at one time or another but something always happened and he was able to get away.

'Peter,' said the trout, 'you're a good boy.'

'To myself be it told,' said Peter. 'But you're the first person who ever said the like.'

'Peter, I'd like you to do me a favour.'

I have you now, thought Peter.

But he said: 'And what would the favour be?'

'Take the hook out of my jaw and put me back in the Turnhole of Creevan.'

'Well, by all that's good,' said Peter, 'if I heard better than that since the day I was born. Put *you* back in the Turnhole. By the Powers Above! Now if you hadn't told me who you were, there might be a chance. But put the Old One back in the water? I'd be the mockery of the whole townland.'

'Peter,' said the Old One, 'I have little time to argue. But put me back into the Turnhole and, by the March Brown and the Mayfly, I'll make it worth your while.'

'You couldn't, and do your best. Always I wanted to catch the Old One, and now I have you.'

But the Old One said: 'Isn't there, now, something you wanted more than to catch me? And I can tell you how to get it. For I have all the wisdom the river whispered to me for a long day before you were born.'

'There is something,' Peter said.

His heart was bouncing with sudden hope.

'There is something. And if you tell me what it

is, and tell me how to get it, then I'll take the hook from your jaw and put you back in the Turnhole of Creevan. But if you tell me a lie, and if you're not the trout I take you for, then I'll drain the Turnhole dry and fry you for the cats.'

The length of line quivered in the grass like a telegraph wire in the wind. Peter knew the trout was trembling. Fish hate cats, I suppose, because cats like fish.

'What you want, Peter, son of Jamesy, the milkman,' said the Old One, 'is to be a man of power, to marry the daughter of a king and to live in a palace forever and ever.'

'True for you, my man in the grass. Now tell me how to set about it.'

'Peter you're a good boy ....'

'You told me that already. And if you are a wise and truthful trout you won't say it again.'

'Then,' said the Old One.

He was speaking in a hurry, one word slipping like water after the other, for even the Old One is enough of a fish to prefer the water in the Turnhole of Creevan to the grass in Creevan meadow.

'Then,' said the Old One, 'this is how you are to set about it. Go along the bank of the river until you come to the Bridge of Drumragh and from the Bridge of Drumragh follow the lane that will lead you across the Hill of Dooish, and cross the Hill of

Dooish until you come to the Stream of Claramore, and follow the Stream of Claramore in the direction of the sea until you come to the house that has neither a door nor a window and the man who lives in the house that has neither a door nor a window will tell you what to do after that.'

'I'll do so,' said Peter. 'But remember, if you've told me a lie ....'

'Trout never lie,' said the Old One.

And Peter felt a wee bit ashamed of himself.

He bent down into the long grass and saw the Old One lying there with never a wriggle out of him. He was worn out with the thirst and with too much talking.

When Peter saw the size of the trout he almost regretted the bargain he had just made. Then he thought of the king's daughter and, gently, he removed the hook from the trout's jaw. The Old One could no longer slither through the grass. So Peter lifted him up, and that was about as much as he could do, and carried him to the water's edge. When he felt the weight of the Old One he once again almost regretted his bargain, but again he thought of the king's daughter, of the joy of being a man of power and living in a palace forever and ever.

So he lowered the Old One into the shallows and held him there for a moment until the cool water brought the life back.

Then he loosened his grip and the Old One slipped from the shallows into the deep water and was gone.

For a moment Peter sat sorrowfully by the river. But when he thought again of the king's daughter he stood up and grasped his switch. The red wriggling worms he emptied into the river. The Old One could now eat and enjoy them without danger. The tin he flung, for good luck, over his left shoulder and into the long grass. Then he turned on his heel as sharp as a soldier and walked along the bank of the river towards the Bridge of Drumragh.

As he walked he sang loudly a song he had heard his mother sing. He didn't know what it meant but he sang it just the same:

'Tidy girly, tidy girly,
Tidy girly always.
Milk the cow in the tail of your gown
And throw it into the saucepan.'

2

With the first sight in the distance of the Bridge of Drumragh Peter discovered that he was hungry.

So when he had climbed the steep path, from the river bank to the road, he took from his pocket the farl of oaten bread his mother had baked for him on the previous day. Sitting on the stone parapet of the bridge he broke the farl into fragments and, because he had no butter or no way to get it, he ate the fragments without butter. Then, rested and refreshed, he went on his way, following the lane to the Hill of Dooish as instructed by the trout. On the far side of the hill he came to a stream. 'This must be the Stream of Claramore,' he said to himself. He began to follow it in the direction of the sea, but it was a long way and he grew tired.

He slept that night in a sheltered glen where the wind talked in the dark with branches of alder and birch and hazel.

In the dawn of the next morning he went on walking beside the stream until a hedge of whitethorn blocked his way. Bursting his way through it, he jumped down a steep bank to a sandy lane leading up and up to the top of a hill. And on the top of that hill stood the house that had neither door nor window.

It was a small whitewashed house, roofed with yellow thatch. Through a hole in the thatch the blue smoke went curling and writing things on the air. A fence of clods without either gateway or gap went all around the house. But it didn't take Peter long to climb up to the top of the fence and jump down on the inside.

He walked up to the house. He walked around it several times. Then he sat down on a flat stone and scratched his head and spoke to himself.

'By all that's good,' he said, 'here's a fix. Sure if the house has no doorway to walk through or no window to see through how am I to speak with the man who lives within. This is the thing that has happened to me for trusting a deceitful trout. One of his breed was never known to tell a true word.'

He was hungry again. He wondered how long a man had to live on bread and water before marrying a king's daughter. He wondered if the king's daughter would be pleased with a very thin husband. Then he noticed the lazy lift of the coiling blue smoke and his heart gave a great leap and his lips a great shout.

He climbed up onto the thatch. On his hands and knees he crawled to the hole which the smoke came from. The smoke set him coughing and made his eyes water but he was able to look down at the inside of the house. He saw a shining oaken settle and a tall dresser. But although he leaned down and forward until he almost fell into the fire he could see only one half of the room. He saw no living person, man, woman or child.

He called and called again: 'Is there anybody down there?'

Nobody answered.

Very angry at this uncivil reception, he gripped the edge of the chimney, if you could call it a chimney, and felt downwards with his feet until they rested on the iron crane on which the kettle and the pots hung over the fire. The heat scorched the soles of his boots. But with a quick sideways spring he jumped clear of the fire to land on his hands and knees in the middle of the floor.

And as he did so a small hunchbacked man came out from behind the dresser, holding a sharp, shining sword, or a long knife or something. You couldn't be sure about it. But whatever it was, he brandished it within an inch of the nose of Peter, the son of Jamesy the milkman.

Never before had Peter laid eyes on such a man. His back was humped and his legs were bent and bowed so badly that they would have fitted around the wheel of a barrow. His head was as large or larger than the biggest head of cabbage Peter had ever seen. He had a flowing black beard. But the hair that grew on his head and hung down over his shoulders was the colour of red gold. He wore a white shirt, a crimson tailed-coat, a pair of green knee-breeches, blue stockings: and his shoes were the colour of his hair.

He was the smallest, strangest, brightest little man that Peter had ever seen. He danced about the floor. He waved his sword, or whatever it was. He seemed, at the same time, to be the bravest and most dangerous man in any part of the world that Peter had ever been in. Not that Peter had seen much of the world up to that moment, as you know as well as I do.

The little man danced to the right and he danced to the left. And all the time he shook the sword, or whatever, and swung it left and right, missing

Peter's nose by inches. On his hands and knees, and with something between amazement and amusement in his heart, Peter wished himself back with the milk cart and the pony. Or, at least, back on the bank of the river in Creevan meadow before that sly trout made a fool of him. But no matter how much he wished and wished, there he still was on his hands and knees on the floor: and the little man still capered, and shook the sword, and screamed in a squeaky voice like the scream of an angry seagull.

'What do you want?' the little man cried.

And on he went: 'Who sent you here?'

And: 'Woe to you, you thief of the early morning. You plundering, roaming, robbing vagabond. Who are you? What do you want?'

Poor Peter, if it were to save his life, could not put two words together, either inside in his mind or on the tip of his tongue. He stayed where he was on his hands and knees. He had nowhere else to go. He opened and closed his mouth, for all the world like a hooked fish. But little by little he recovered from his surprise and, little by little, his natural courage came filtering back.

When he saw that the little man had no intention of making use of the sword, or whatever it was, he stood up ....

Well, he knelt up. You couldn't stand up in that

house, if you were the size of Peter, without putting your head out through the hole in the thatch.

So, he knelt up and he said: 'The Trout in the Turnhole of Creevan sent me to ask you if ....'

'What you, by you, with you, from you, where you, when you, before you, behind you, for you, against you, yes you, no you,' the little man screamed.

He danced on one leg. He whistled the sword, or whatever it was, around his head until it sang like a branch in the wind. But by and by he settled down. It was plain to see that the name of the Old One was having some effect on him.

He leaned on the sword, or whatever it was. Long and hard he looked at Peter. Then he said: 'The Trout in the Turnhole of Creevan is an honest man, a credit to his generation.'

Said Peter: 'Which is his generation?'

The little man leaned so heavily on his sword that he drove the blade deep into the earthen floor. Then he seated himself on the crosshandled hilt ....

So it must have been a sword.

He seated himself on the crosshandled hilt. He settled his legs like a tailor squatting on the floor, the way tailors do. He placed his elbows on his knees and his chin and beard on his two hands. He closed his eyes and began to think. The black beard flowed over his hands and down to the floor.

He thought for a long, long time. So long that Peter thought that he had been forgotten about. So he sat down on the oaken settle and stretched his big feet out to toast them at the jumping flames of the fire. He was cold and hungry and tired. He closed his eyes to sleep. He thought he might as well. But then the little man suddenly spoke.

He said: 'None know.'

'Know what?' Peter asked.

'None know his generation. All the wise men at the court of a king once gave thought to the matter.

But none of them ever found the answer. The king himself thought ....'

'And the daughter of the king,' said Peter. 'What did she think?'

'The daughters of kings never think. They don't have to.'

Peter blushed and stammered. He was trying to say that he was sorry to be so ignorant as not to know that the daughters of kings never had to think. But the little man looked at him as if he had already forgotten that they had been talking about wise men and a king and the daughter of a king.

He said: 'You tell me that the Trout in the Turnhole of Creevan sent you here to talk to me. But how did a fool of a fellow like yourself make the acquaintance of the Trout in the Turnhole of Creevan?'

'I caught him.'

'You caught him?'

With the force of the shock and surprise the little man hopped up and down on the hilt of his sword. Then he said again, and very slowly and very loudly:

'You ... *caught* ... *the Old One*.'

'I did so.'

'And how was the great deed done?'

'With a rod and line.'

'And a hook?'

'And a hook.'

The little man took his hands and his arms out of his long, black beard, and waved them around him with excitement. He leaped from his perch on the hilt of the sword and came forward to the fire. He sat down beside Peter on the settle. He invited Peter to make himself at home.

Home, Peter thought, was never like this.

'And tell me now. What happened when you landed the Trout?'

'I let him go. I put him back in the Turnhole of Creevan.'

The little fellow looked sideways at Peter. There was black suspicion in his eyes. He seemed to be thinking that he had heard that one before.

So Peter said: 'On two conditions I let him go. That he would tell me what it was that I wanted most in the world. And that he would tell me how to get it. Then he sent me to you to ask you the best way to become a man of power, to marry the daughter of a king and to live in a palace forever and ever.'

The little man took his right knee between his hands and rocked himself gently backward and forward. The skin of his forehead was so puckered up with thought and puzzlement that it almost vanished under his red as gold hair.

'Who are you?' he asked.

Peter told him who he was and where he came from.

'Well, Peter, you deserve well to marry the daughter of a king. You were clever enough to catch the Old One and he has all the wisdom of running water. And you were kind enough to let him go.

'But, Peter, there are dangers in the way. I suppose the daughter of an ordinary rich man would not do.'

'No,' said Peter.

'Too bad, too bad,' said the little man. 'For in these days the daughters of kings are few and far between.'

Thinking harder and harder he rocked faster and faster. He thought so hard and he rocked so fast that in the end he rocked from the settle to the floor. So he stayed sitting on the floor. His black beard coiled like a snake in the round space between his crooked legs. He put his head between his hands and went on thinking as hard as ever.

At long last he said: 'Peter, if you are the man for the job, I can think of one king's daughter. But there are great dangers in the way.'

'What dangers?' said Peter.

He stood up on his knees. He turned his back to the fire. He looked very brave.

'First of all you must help me to climb out of this

house. For here I am a prisoner until the man comes who is brave enough to dare ....'

'To dare what?' said Peter. 'To dare whom?'

He felt like leaping up and shouting but he had to remember to stay on his knees.

'Tell me the whole story,' he said. 'For at this moment I fear no man nor his mother.'

3

The little man opened his mouth to speak, but no words came out. Whatever he had intended to say seemed to be frozen on his lips.

He put his ear to the floor as if he were listening. When he stood up again his eyes were jumping with terror.

He shouted or screamed, or whatever you like to call it. He was a very little man and he wasn't much good at the shout: 'Peter, do you hear anything?'

Peter put his right ear to the floor. He heard a sound like the sound made by a retreating wave on the strand or shore at Tullaghan when the great grey stones and blue stones are swept along by the waves and rubbed against each other until they are as round and smooth as chestnuts.

Closer and closer came the sound. Then he heard the splash of water, the snapping of breaking boughs, the swift whirr in the air as startled birds went by.

Some terrible thing had crossed the stream of

Claramore and was coming towards them through the woods.

Peter gripped the little man by the shoulder. He asked him what was happening. He asked him what awful thing was thundering towards them, splashing through streams, smashing through woods, frightening the birds from their nests on the branches.

But the little man's lips were shaking with panic and he couldn't speak a word. So Peter, feeling that something must be done, caught the sword and pulled it out of the earthen floor. He cleaned it on his trousers, such as they were, very tattered by this time. He bent the sword with his two hands. He shook the sword in the air just as if he had played with swords in his cradle; although, to tell you the truth, he had never handled a sword until that moment.

Closer and closer came the sound.

Peter could now tell that it was not a wave of the sea. Nor was it thunder, nor a high wind.

It was a man walking. He had to be a big man, a huge man, a monstrous man. He had to be a giant. He came thumping along on feet as big as steamrollers until the earth shook, and the walls of the little hole of a house shook, and the plates fell from the dresser and smashed or rolled around the floor.

And just when
Peter was sure and
certain that the
house was going
to fall down, the
noise stopped as
suddenly as it had
begun.
But Peter, and I suppose
the little man as well, who
were inside the house, felt
the air grow warm as if a
man as high as the sky,
with clouds around his head
and the sun on his shoulders,
was bending down above the
house and blowing his burning
breath on the thatch. The smoke
from the fire blew back down
the hole in the roof and set
Peter and the little man
coughing and spluttering,
and their eyes watering.
A loud voice spoke, rumbling
in the air as far above them as
the song the lark sings in the
bright morning. And this is
what they heard:

'You have another man in there, you little rascal. Is it trying to escape you are? I'll escape you. Meelamor will escape you. Come up and out, come up and out, the two of you. Or by the seven daughters of seven kings baked in seven pies and eaten without salt, I'll sit on the thatch and flatten you. I'll bring the walls down on your heads and shoulders.'

The words died away into a harsh laugh that ran and rattled up into the heavens like fading thunder.

Peter waved the sword about his head insofar as

he could wave it in the confined space. He tried to think of something nasty to shout back through the hole in the thatch. But when he looked at the little man and saw the tears rolling down his face, his courage failed him.

'We may as well go out,' said the little man. 'It will save the house, at least. It may be of use to somebody when we're dead and gone.'

So Peter gave him a leg up from the settle to the crane. Then he gave him another leg up from the crane to the edge of the hole in the roof. And from the edge of the hole in the roof the little man was whipped away like a wisp of straw caught in a tempest of wind.

With his heart between his teeth with fear, but with the sword still in his hand, Peter climbed after him. He crawled out onto the thatch. He looked up. He saw the giant.

The giant, Meelamor, was as tall as a beechtree. He was as stout as a sycamore or an old oak. He was as lithe and supple as the brown birch that grows in the bog.

When Peter sat down on the thatched roof and looked up he thought that he himself was a very small fellow indeed.

But he wasn't given much time to feel either small or large. For Meelamor reached down and

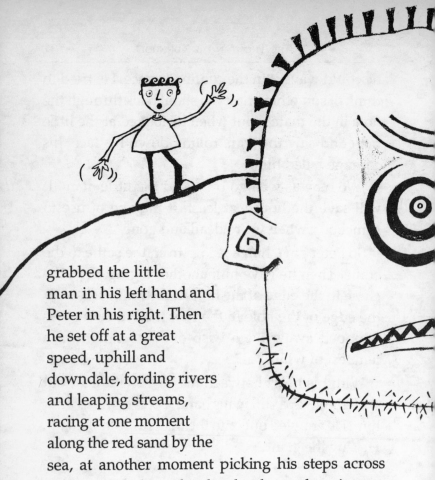

grabbed the little
man in his left hand and
Peter in his right. Then
he set off at a great
speed, uphill and
downdale, fording rivers
and leaping streams,
racing at one moment
along the red sand by the
sea, at another moment picking his steps across
quaggy, shaking bogland where the air was
pierced by the lonely cry of the curlew and the
cackling cry of the snipe.

Meelamor swung his long arms slowly when he
walked, and he swung them quickly when he ran, so
that Peter and the little man went up and down, up
and down, with the wind whistling in their ears, for
all the world as if they had been tied around the waist
in two long ropes and set swinging far up in the air.

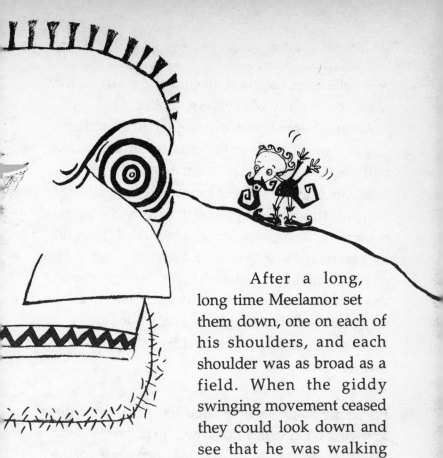

After a long, long time Meelamor set them down, one on each of his shoulders, and each shoulder was as broad as a field. When the giddy swinging movement ceased they could look down and see that he was walking along a wide road paved with smooth stones and winding gently down into a wooded valley. A river flowed down the middle of the valley. On the bank of the river a grey gloomy castle raised its towers until they were lost in the racing clouds.

Meelamor's great strides brought them swiftly towards the castle. Now and again and to shorten the distance he left the winding road and stepped across fields and forests as easily as an ordinary man would step over a tuft of grass. Very soon he was following the road around the walls of the castle to the place where the gate was.

Although Meelamor was the tallest giant Peter had ever seen he still looked small when compared with those walls and tottering, dizzy towers.

Through great gates of brass that clanged shut behind them, they passed into a deserted courtyard. And there Meelamor picked them off his shoulders as if they were insects. He set them on the ground. He blew his hot breath around them. He laughed like thunder when they staggered like men caught in a high wind.

Then he left them there and went his own way into the castle.

For a long time they wandered about in silence, not knowing what to say nor where to go nor what to do. They were afraid to leave the open spaces of the courtyard and approach the surrounding buildings. For in those buildings there might be dogs or cats belonging to Meelamor: cats as big as ponies and dogs the size of horses.

As well as that they were afraid that some of the giant's servants might come upon them and grab them and beat them or bake them into a pie. And although neither the little man nor Peter had much hope of escaping alive from that castle they, naturally, wanted to postpone the end as long as they could. While they were still alive there was always a little hope.

They heard neither bark nor snarl nor the sound of voices nor footsteps. They heard nothing at all but the whistle of the wind far aloft in the chinks and crannies of those terrible towers. They were hungry, cold and miserable. Weary and sick at heart they sat down to rest, somewhat sheltered from the cold wind by a huge pillar that stood in the centre of the courtyard. Everything in this fearful place had to be huge.

And the weather in this place, wherever it is, thought Peter, isn't in the least like the sunny weather in Creevan meadow. Only he was too miserable for anger, or for anything but misery, he would have hated the sly, talking trout, now laughing, for sure, at the foolishness of fishermen, and frisking his fine tail in the deep, cool water of the Turnhole.

'My wee man,' he said, 'my wee rainbow of a man, would you mind telling me where we are.'

That was a silly question. It did not deserve and it did not get an answer. For Peter knew as well as you or I that they were prisoners in the Castle of Meelamor and that they hadn't a hope of escape.

The little man rocked his body backward and forward and moaned with sorrow. Listening carefully to his lament Peter made out these words, repeated again and again and again:

'Sad is this fate for one who once lived in the palace of a king ... Sad is this fate for one who once lived in the palace of a king ....'

'And do you tell me,' said Peter, 'is it the like of you, meaning no offence, that ever saw the inside of the palace of a king?'

Then the little man ceased the moaning. He replied in a firm, clear voice: 'My name is Beg. By right of birth and by talent I was once the official maker of jokes at the court of a great king. The name of the king was Rory and he ruled over a southern country beside the sea. The sun shines brighter there, the birds sing sweeter songs, the perfume of the flowers is more fragrant than in any other land that is known to men.'

So Peter asked him how did it come about that he left that happy land to live in a hovel that had no windows to catch the sun and no door where he could sit in the dusk of the long summer evenings to hear the birds sing.

'That's a long and bitter tale,' said Beg. 'And there are many things in it that you could never understand. So I'll shorten it when I tell it to you.'

4

This was the story that Beg told Peter as they sat, sheltering behind the pillar from the icy wind, in the courtyard before the castle of Meelamor.

'King Rory was a just man. But he had a fierce enemy and an unfaithful friend.

'That unfaithful friend was his own sister. The fierce enemy was the giant, Meelamor. And the friend and the enemy came together to plot the destruction of the king.

'The name of the king's sister was Edda and she had the powers of a witch. By her black spells she changed the king into a poor man and drove him out of the palace to wander the earth and work as a labourer. When he was gone, Meelamor became king, and for a long time no flowers grew, no birds sang, and the sun never shone on the southern country by the sea.

'But the people of the land rose up in anger and chased Meelamor to the east and Edda to the west, and to this day they hold the Kingdom for Rory until he returns.'

So Peter wanted to know why he didn't return.

'The spells that the wicked woman put on him,' said the little man. 'He has forgotten who he is.

Nobody knows where he is except Edda. And she keeps that knowledge in her own evil heart. Even if we could find him, there is only one way to remove the spells. And only one man who would be able to do so.'

'Who is he?'

'I don't know.'

'You don't know. You're in a bad way so. You don't know where the king is. You don't know who the man is who could remove the spells. The king, wherever he is, doesn't know who he is. It's a bad job.'

'It is, indeed.'

'The only thing we do know is where we are,' said Peter. 'And that's twice as bad a job.'

The little man shivered. He said: 'It's very cold.'

'It won't worry us much longer,' said Peter. He

stood up to walk around to warm
himself. But he waited for a while
to hear the end of the wee fellow's
story.

'When Rory was driven
out from his kingdom he

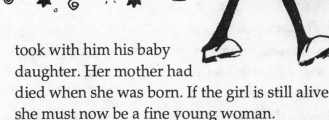

took with him his baby
daughter. Her mother had
died when she was born. If the girl is still alive
she must now be a fine young woman.

The man who meets her and loves her enough to
risk his life for her can remove the spells from her
father by laying his hand on the king's head and
signing him with the sign of the cross.

'But if the girl is now dead, then all hope is gone.'

Peter stood silent for a long time, his mind deep in
the sadness of that story.

Tear followed tear down the funny, furrowed
face of the little man.

'And why,' Peter asked him, 'did you come

into this land?'

'I came looking for the king because there was a rumour that he had travelled this way. But I didn't find him. Instead Meelamor found me and made me a prisoner in the house that has neither door nor window. And now the pair of us are prisoners in this dreadful castle.'

Then Peter did a surprising thing. Standing up straight and stretching out his arms he laughed until the tears ran down his face as fast as the tears of sorrow ran down the deep wrinkles into Beg's black beard.

Beg looked at him in terror. For he thought that the fear of death had turned Peter's head and set him laughing mad.

'Beg,' said Peter, 'it makes me laugh to think that it's you and I against Meelamor and Edda and the whole world. Still, it's a true thing to say that while we live we are alive and that we're not dead until we die. I'm alive and I'm hungry and I'll eat before I do anything else.'

He turned quickly for, from a distance, he heard light steps approaching across the cobbles of the courtyard.

'Look, Beg. Someone's coming. And it's not Meelamor.'

Beg looked up. He saw a young girl coming across the courtyard.

'Nor is it Edda,' he said.

'Then,' said Peter, 'it might be the daughter of a king.'

So he ran across the courtyard to meet the advancing maiden. Beg looked after him. And saw that, as the boy and the girl came closer to each other, Peter halted, raised his hand to his head and cried out in amazement.

For the girl walking across the courtyard was no princess. She was Kate, the daughter of a poor farmer called Shawn, and every night when she dreamed she saw Peter in her dreams.

Peter led the girl to the place where the little man sat in the shelter of the pillar.

He was silent with disappointment. He had run to meet he knew not whom and he had found only Kate. But when a sidelong glance showed him that tears were streaming down the girl's face his heart softened.

'Peter,' she said, between her sobs, 'it's a sad chance has brought us to meet here. Meelamor has ordered me to bring the two of you into the castle and to give you some food.'

When Peter heard that he was back again in good humour.

'Well now, Kate,' he said, 'things are not as bad as they might be. Taken as a whole the day may be sad. But there's nothing wrong with the hour that brings me the promise of food. For, by all that's good, I'm away in the head with hunger. And as for Beg, the little bit of appetite he has room for is gaping like an angry gander.'

Gently he helped the tired little man to his feet. They turned towards the castle.

'Lead us to the food, Kate,' Peter said. 'And as we go tell us how you happen to be here.'

'What is there to tell?' she cried. 'We were taken here against our will.'

'We ...,' said Peter.

'My father and myself. We were taken here by Meelamor.'

Your father as well as yourself. And where is he now?'

'I don't know.'

Kate sobbed.

'He was taken away from me when we got here. I haven't laid eyes on him since. I don't know whether he's dead or alive.'

'This is, indeed, a very sad story,' Beg said.

That was the first time he had spoken to Kate. He gave her a long, hard, curious look. He said: 'And what do you do here in the Castle?'

'Meelamor has made me the servant of everybody who lives in the castle. They keep me working from morning to night.'

'And how many people do live here?'

'Well now,' Kate said.

She was counting on her fingers that were hacked and rough from cooking and cleaning and scrubbing and polishing.

'There's Meelamor and Edda, and the rest of us are prisoners, my father, if he's still alive, and myself and the princess ....'

Peter and Beg said suddenly and together: 'The princess. The daughter of a king.'

'She says she is,' said Kate.

She tilted her head and sniffed with disdain.

'But she never told me what king was her father. Or where he reigns. Or whether he reigns at all, or not.'

Beg and Peter exchanged a wise look. But they said nothing. For they both thought that Kate would never understand the idea that was in their heads.

And at that moment they passed through a high arched doorway into the big cold castle.

They walked along high and windy passages, vaulted and paved and walled with grey stone.

They went up along winding flights of solid stone stairs.

They came at last to an enormous room. In the middle of the room there was a long table of rough splintered wood. The walls were hung with black cloths which waved and billowed in draughts of wind that were violent enough to blow an ordinary house clear from its foundations.

But this was not an ordinary house. Everything was huge: walls and doors and windows. They had to shout to make themselves heard. The echoes of their voices were lost in the rafters which seemed to be as far away as heaven.

Peter and Beg sat down on stools at an ordinary sort of a table close to a roaring fire in a corner of the room. Strong as the draughts were the fire was still bright enough to make them feel warm and comfortable, and the table was made to suit their size and laid to suit their hunger.

While they sat eating Kate left them. She hadn't returned when they had finished eating. They were feeling so warm and full and satisfied that they had almost forgotten where they were and the fate that might lie in store for them. They drew their stools closer to the fire. They sat down to smoke and chat. Where did they get the tobacco? Kate had given it to them.

Only then did they notice that there was another person in the room.

She sat quietly in a sheltered chimney corner. The very first moment Peter saw her he said to himself that that was the princess, the daughter of the king.

No doubt at all about it, she was beautiful. Her dark hair was parted in the middle and fell down glossy and gleaming over the back of the chair she sat on. Her skin was lovely and brown. Her profile was clear and firm. She was dressed in a loose, flowing robe of dark, rich cloth, and around her neck and on her arms she wore precious jewels and ornaments of gold.

But, somehow, her face was sullen and pettish in a way that did harm to her beauty. And Peter was timid in her presence and wondered how he would open the conversation.

But Beg solved that problem and put an end to Peter's wondering. Beg had no doubt in the world as to who the young woman was. To Peter he muttered some words about family likeness. Then he ran forward and went down on one knee. And she reached out her right hand in great style. And reverently Beg put it to his lips.

'You are Beg,' she said. 'I am waiting on you for a long, long time.'

To the ears of the faithful little man her voice was as sweet as the song of the first bird of the Spring.

'And you,' he said, 'are my mistress and my queen, the daughter of King Rory.'

'Oh, Beg! how often did my father speak of you before ... before ....'

And all of a sudden the beautiful girl began to cry as if her heart were breaking.

Beg waited until the first storm had passed. His little wrinkled face was twice as wrinkled with puzzlement. Then he asked: 'Before what? Where is King Rory now?'

The princess said that she did not know. Very prettily, she wiped her eyes with little dabs of a tiny, silk handkerchief.

'Don't ask me,' she said, 'for I don't know. He was taken away, and now I do not know whether he is alive or dead. Don't ask me to speak of the past. It's far too sad. Let us think only of the present. You are here now and we can die together.'

Now, in spite of the good meal that was under his belt and in spite of the heat of the fire that was warm as a sun in June, Peter shivered when he heard that. He had no wish to die at any time. Least of all when he had just laid his eyes on the beautiful daughter of a king.

'Daughter of King Rory,' he said.

You see he didn't know her name, and even if he had known it, he still would not have known how to say it.

'Daughter of King Rory. We won't talk more than we can help about death or dying.'

He raised his right arm in the air and shook his fist. It was a good big fist. He said: 'I'd do a lot even against a giant before I'd see you suffer harm.'

The princess looked at him suspiciously. She asked Beg who this fellow might be. She was very haughty.

'He is my good friend, Peter,' Beg said. 'He is a wise boy and a brave boy. You could trust Peter with your life.'

The words came straight from the honest heart of the little man. Then the princess smiled and reached out her hand to Peter. He bowed as well as he could. He wasn't much used to bowing. And he kissed the hand of the beautiful daughter of the king.

They couldn't talk about the present because it wasn't cheerful. They couldn't talk about the future because they might never live to see it. But Beg, like a man in a lovely dream, talked about the great days of the past when King Rory had ruled in power and everyone had been happy: happy people walking on the roads and working in the fields, happy birds singing on sunny branches, the happy colours of the flowers, and the sun all day long shining from a cloudless blue sky.

These were all beautiful things to hear about and to think about.

Listening to Beg's words Peter was almost able to forget the windy prison of a castle, and somewhere in some room the terrible giant, Meelamor. They were all in his power.

Peter wondered then would they ever escape. Was King Rory living or dead? Would he ever return again and bring them all with him to the southern country by the warm sea? And what share would Peter himself have in all that good fortune?

For now that he had seen and spoken with the king's daughter he hadn't much hope left of winning her heart and living in a palace forever and ever. For there was something proud and distant in the eyes of the princess when she looked at Peter.

The way of it is, he thought to himself, that she knows by looking at me that I'm no hero nor no prince. I'm nothing but the son of a milkman who stole away from a day's work. I was lucky enough to catch a talking trout but fool enough to listen to his slippery lies. And now I'm here in a muddle that isn't even my business.

Just as he was feeling very sorry for himself the door of the room opened and Kate returned.

It was clear that Kate didn't like the look of the gathering around the fire.

She came towards them very slowly, a frown on her face: and when the princess, glancing over her shoulder, saw Kate she stood up quickly and walked away and out of the long hall. She didn't, Peter thought, even say goodbye. The two young women met and passed each other without speaking. Compared with the beauty of the princess, poor Kate looked more shabby than ever.

'Come with me now,' she said to Beg and Peter.

Her voice sounded cold and uncivil. She led the way along the hall and, meekly, they followed her up another flight of stairs. This time it was a short and narrow flight. Then they came into a twisting sloping passage that seemed to be leading up into the high turrets of the castle. Once Kate stopped before a low opening in the wall. Beg and Peter followed her example. They looked through that opening and found, to their surprise, that they were looking down into the great hall they had just left.

As they looked, a door at the far end of the hall opened and in came Meelamor. After him, very stiff and proud and stately, came Edda, the wife of Meelamor and the wicked sister of King Rory.

Never in all his life, thought Peter, had he seen a

woman who looked so wicked. And in her presence
Meelamor did not look half the size he had seemed
to be when he had raced across the country with Beg
in one hand and Peter in the other.

She was tall and well shaped. She had long dark
hair. She would have passed for beautiful if it
hadn't been for the hard line of her mouth and the
cruel glitter in her black eyes. The thought
suddenly came to Peter that if it hadn't been for the
mouth and eyes, and the difference in age, Edda
would have been very like the young princess. But
then he remembered that since Edda was the sister
of King Rory she must also be the aunt of the
beautiful princess. Between the aunt and the niece
there had to be a family likeness.

He shuddered at the very thought. He hoped
wildly that the likeness did not go beyond the
outward appearance.

Then the voice
of Kate broke in on
his thoughts. She
said:

'You will sleep in the room yonder. The one with the red door.'

She pointed up the long, sloping passage.

'The door isn't locked. But you needn't think there's any chance of escape from the castle. And, sure, maybe you don't want to escape. Now that you're so friendly with the princess.'

With that she turned and left them. They were sorry they had offended her. They hadn't meant to. But at the same time they couldn't help thinking she was a bit silly to be so easily offended.

Anyway they started talking about the princess and planning an escape. They soon forgot about poor, ragged, untidy Kate.

5

Their room was a small one, high up in the highest tower of the castle. Through a hole in the wall, light and air came in, and so did the wind and the rain. Far below they could see the waving tops of the trees and, nearer, under the walls of the castle, the great river they had crossed earlier in the day. It was a wide dark river.

The room was cold and their sleep was broken and disturbed.

At midnight Peter was awake and shivering from the chill air. The sword of Beg hidden under the mattress had left bruises on his back.

He slipped from his bed and looked out through the hole in the wall.

A great round moon was coming up in the sky and the tops of the trees stood stiff and dark against the red glow. The night was bright but cold and lonesome. So he turned away from the hole in the wall and walked across the room to where Beg lay sleeping and snoring. He caught the little man by the shoulder and shook him awake.

'Are you cold?' he said.

That was a foolish question. He could hear the little man's teeth chattering.

'Cold, is it?' said Beg.

With his two hands he was trying to steady his rattling jaws.

'Cold, is it? Cold? Why did you wake me, you head of a fool? Cold? Did you expect me to be warm in this windy barracks? Oh, wisha. If I was only back again in my little house that had neither door nor window, my lovely warm little prison.'

'Prison,' said Peter. 'That reminds me of something. I wonder where in the castle is Kate's father kept a prisoner?'

Beg flapped his arms, trying to warm himself. He said: 'I

don't know and I don't care. But I hope for his own sake he's in a warmer place than this.'

'I wonder is he living or dead. And if he's living, why isn't Kate allowed to see him?'

'It's a puzzle,' Beg said.

'And I'm going to solve it.' Peter walked towards the door of the room.

Beg asked him how he would solve the puzzle.

'I'm going to search until I find him. And if you come with me, you might warm yourself in the search.'

So, Peter leading the way, they slipped from the room and tiptoed for a long time along dark silent corridors, and up and down stairways and, very cautiously, from one room to another. They saw nobody. They heard nobody. And, as far as they could tell, nobody heard them or saw them.

After a while Peter stopped and gripped Beg's arm and said: 'Where exactly are we going?'

'I don't know and I don't care,' Beg said. 'We're keeping warm.'

'Where exactly is Kate's father?'

'How should I know?'

'Then where exactly are we going to search?'

That was a problem. For a long time Beg meditated in the dark silence. Then he said: 'Sure, all we can do is search everywhere.'

Leaning his little weight against a door that was near to him, he pushed it open and bounded through to the room inside.

And in there, before a dying fire, Meelamor sat slumbering. Several empty bottles, each one as big as a barrel, were lined along the mantelpiece. A golden goblet, as big as a tub, lay on the floor at his feet. He snored and grunted and mumbled and muttered in his drunken sleep.

Beg bounded out again, closed the door and fled, but not before Peter had seen the prostrate giant. Running through the darkness to overtake Beg,

Peter thought to himself that no matter how strong a man was he was always liable to meet somebody or something stronger than himself. The thought gave him more courage than he had had since the moment when it dawned on him that he had caught the Old One.

Before another closed door, Beg, breathless, stopped running.

'That was a near thing,' he said.

'It was,' said Peter. 'But our search isn't over yet.'

Very slowly, with great caution, and without making a single sound, he opened the door.

There before them was the great courtyard. The moon and the stars were glittering in the high sky. In the distance the river-water rippled. The wind, moving gently in the branches of the trees along the river, was no longer rough and loud.

'You go that way,' Peter said.

He pointed towards one end of the courtyard.

'Keep an eye out to find if there's any way we can escape from this place. I'll go towards the river. And when the moon is on the top of that tall tree, we will meet again. Here. At this door.'

With that he walked off and Beg, too, went his own way walking, as much as he could, in the shelter of the shadows cast by the high walls of the castle.

Before long Peter came to a corner of the castle where the cobbled courtyard ended. There before him was a place of rough, tangled grass and stunted trees. Slipping into the shadow of the trees he went feeling his way from trunk to trunk until he came at last to the edge of the moving water.

Every ripple shone white on the top with the light of the moon and was dark in the hollow with its own shadow; seeing all that flowing and flashing and changing, his eyes were dazzled as if all the jewels in the world had been shown to him at one time. And while he was blinking his eyes and trying to see if it might be possible to wade or swim across the river, the voice spoke to him: 'So there you are, Peter.'

That was what it said.

For a moment he thought that it was the voice of somebody hiding in the long grass or in the black shadows under the trees. It might be a spy sent by Meelamor. It was a strange slippery voice. He had heard it somewhere before.

Then he remembered and he knew.

So he bent down until his lips almost touched the passing water. He said in a sharp angry voice: 'Is it come to mock me you are? You may well be content with the trouble your lying tales have landed me into.'

He stared hard into the water but he could see

neither the Old One, nor anything nor anybody else. That cunning trout was hiding somewhere behind a stone. But Peter could hear the voice clearly.

'Peter,' said the Old One, 'I told you before now that trout never lie.'

'You told me nonsense.'

'Is this all the thanks you have for me that has travelled many a weary mile to help you?'

'By the Powers,' said Peter, 'but that beats all. Here am I lost forever because I followed your advice. And you have the hard neck to ask me to be grateful.'

'Peter,' said the Old One, 'may I remind you that trout do not have necks.'

Peter was embarrassed. He had to admit that that was the truth. But he blustered on: 'Didn't I ask you to help me to find the daughter of a king ....'

'And didn't I do so? Haven't you found her?'

'I have, indeed. And black sorrow be on the day that first brought her before my eyes. Here. In the castle of Meelamor.'

'There's a way out.'

'Is that so, now?' said Peter. 'Then I'll be mighty grateful if you tell me where it is. But, sure, even if we were out and free the princess wouldn't look across the road at me. She's rotten with pride.'

'She's what?' said the Old One.

He must have been opening and closing his gills at a great rate. Peter could clearly hear the gurgle. That's what trout do when they're surprised and puzzled. They can't very well scratch their heads.

'What did you say she was?'

'Rotten with pride.'

'You're making a great mistake, my boy. Speaking as an honest trout I can tell you she's a fine girl. And what's more ... she's fond of you.'

Very bitterly Peter said: 'I don't doubt you at all. But, speaking for myself, I think I'd get along better with Kate who is only the daughter of a poor farmer.'

'What did you say, boy?'

'With Kate, the daughter of Shawn, who's a poor farmer and a prisoner here in this castle.'

'If you don't mind me telling you so, Peter,' said the Old One, 'there's as much sense in your big head as in one of your father's milk cans.'

'I'm delighted to hear that,' said Peter.

He thought that if he could see the trout and grab him he'd shake manners into his skin for a year, or shake the life out of him.

But the slippery voice went on talking: 'All the same you're not a bad fellow. So sit down on the bank and I'll tell you a story. And don't open your mouth or speak a word until I've finished.'

6

When the moon was sitting on the top of the tall tree Peter came, silent and thoughtful, back to the little side door of the castle. Beg was waiting, hiding in the shadows.

In silence they made their way back to their own cold room. There, in the dark, Beg spoke miserably.

'I found no way out,' he said.

'Maybe you didn't want to,' said Peter.

'What do you mean?' poor Beg said.

He was shivering with cold, and cold with surprise.

'It's fond of the place you're getting,' Peter said. 'You and your fancy princess. She's a bargain, indeed. Much good may she do you.'

In the dark he heard Beg muttering angrily. 'That's no way to speak of your betters. And you only the son of a milkman.'

And not another word did he speak. But he lay breathing heavily, a very angry, funny little man.

Peter pulled the bedclothes up to his chin, and

for a long, long time he shook with silent laughter.

The sun came up over the tops of the trees and warmed the walls of their room.

Peter awoke. In the hush of the morning he stole silently from his bed. As he passed out of the room he smiled down on poor little Beg who lay sound asleep and snoring, his mouth wide open and his black beard outside the blankets.

Peter went down the long sloping corridor, down the steep stairs, and down past the door of the great hall in which, last night, they had met the princess. He went down and down until he came to the basement and the cellars. And the dungeons.

Through an open doorway came the sound of splashing and the bubbling noises made by a boiling pot, a very big pot. In there he knew he would find Kate busy preparing breakfast for everybody in the castle. He tiptoed to the open doorway. But the sound of voices halted him. Kate was not alone.

Cautiously he peeped into the room. He saw Kate and the princess. They were quarrelling.

'So you want to know where I am going, Miss Kate, the Scullion,' said the princess. 'Then let me tell you that I'm going to do the duty that the master of the house wouldn't trust you to do. Because of your low birth and breeding.'

'My birth and breeding might be as good as yours,' Kate answered.

She turned her back on the princess.

She said: 'Go on now about your business. I've no intention of following you. I have work to do.'

'And well the work suits you,' said the princess.

High and haughty she walked away from Kate. She was carrying a tray.

She crossed the steaming kitchen towards a door in the opposite wall. Swinging on her belt as she walked were two keys, a large one and a small one. With the large key she opened the door.

'Shut it carefully,' Kate said, 'in case I follow you.'

The princess looked back over her shoulder and laughed in scorn.

'I'll leave it open,' she said. 'Follow me if you dare. But if you do I wouldn't like to be in your shoes when Meelamor comes roaring for his breakfast.'

Then the princess was gone. The door stood open behind her. Like a flash, and before the astonished Kate could halt him, Peter was across the kitchen and through the doorway. He followed the footsteps of the proud princess.

He was in a long, dismal corridor. It wasn't so high, since he must have been halfway down to the centre of the earth, so it wasn't as windy as the parts

of the castle he had already seen. The walls were by no means smooth, and rough pillars and buttresses, curtained and clothed in black cobwebs, were here, there and everywhere. He saw a few spiders and they seemed to him to be as big as footballs. It's hard to say with spiders; so much of them is legs. But they looked at him as he passed. He was sure of that.

Thirty or forty yards ahead the princess had paused. From a hole in the wall she took a tall candle and a flint. She lighted the candle and held it in her right hand, balancing the tray on her left.

She was very skilful. On she went. Dodging from pillar to buttress and from buttress to pillar, Peter followed.

Down and down and down. For a while there was a shadowy, grey light but as they went deeper the light failed and Peter found it hard to see where he was going or what was under his feet. But he stumbled along as well as he could, keeping his eyes firmly fixed on the fluttering flame of the candle that went before him in the dark like a great golden butterfly. Down and down until the air was dead and heavy, and he longed for the green grass of Creevan meadow, and the blue sky, and the south wind.

But every journey must end sometime. That journey ended when the princess stopped and knelt down to fix the candle, and settle the tray securely on the ground. Hiding in the darkness, behind a cold rough pillar, Peter watched her. The light of the candle shone on a large iron door and the princess was fumbling a key into the lock.

Then, with a great clanking of bolts and a creaking of hinges, and a rattling of rusty chains along the hard ground, the door swung open. The princess picked up the candle and the tray and went through the doorway.

Holding his breath, and stepping quietly as a cat on the very tips of his toes, Peter went closer and closer to the open door until he could see into the place beyond. And this is what he saw by the golden, flickering light of the candle:

A tall man standing in the middle of a dungeon.

A tall man with grey hair and broad shoulders.

A handsome man with firm mouth and jaw, and wide smooth forehead.

A man fastened by heavy chains to the dripping wall of the dungeon.

The man was Shawn, the poor farmer, the father of Kate.

He moved a step forward and the heavy chains rattled. He stood still, his eyes blinking, dazzled by the light of the candle. He put his right hand to his forehead. In his eyes and around his mouth there was an appearance of loneliness. He was like a man exiled a long time from his own country.

Peter saw all that in one quick glance while the princess was bending down to put the tray on the floor. Then, before she could turn around to leave the dungeon, he headed back like a ghost to the kitchen where Kate was guarding the door. His eyes were used to the darkness by now and he went quickly and quietly along the rough tunnel. He didn't even take time to speak to Kate. But he touched her lips with his forefinger as he ran across the great, steaming kitchen. Kate was happy then because she knew she shared a secret with Peter. It was her desire always to have even a little part of all his secrets.

Peter went up and up to the windy room where Beg was still peacefully sleeping. He didn't waken Beg. He just sat down on the edge of his own bed. He put his chin on his hands and thought and thought until he gave himself a pain in the head.

An hour afterwards, when Beg was rubbing the

sleep out of his eyes, Kate came into the room. Her eyes were red as if she had been crying.

'Meelamor has ordered me to bring the two of you into his presence,' she said. 'As soon as you've broken your fast.'

In a very bitter voice little Beg said: 'he's mighty considerate. It was kind of him to think that we might be hungry.'

'He wanted me to tell him if you ever thought of making your escape.'

'Well, well,' said Peter. 'You should have told him that Beg likes the castle so well that he wouldn't dream of leaving it. Not even if the walls fell down.'

At that the face of Beg grew so red with anger that nobody could say where his forehead ended and his bright hair began. Peter laughed aloud. Kate looked at them with puzzled eyes. She wondered why Beg was angry and Peter laughing. Not knowing what to say she wisely said nothing.

When they had eaten their breakfast she led them to another room where Meelamor and Edda sat together on high chairs. Meelamor's chair was down in a hole in the floor so that his big hairy knees were level with the floor and his face almost, but not quite on a level with Edda's face.

But Peter thought of the drunken giant he had seen the night before and his fear vanished. Red

wine could conquer Meelamor, and Peter's mother
had always told him that a brave heart was
stronger than red wine. So he took the lead and
strode like a hero up the room until he came to the
place where the giant and his wicked wife were
sitting. He shouted up at Meelamor: 'What do you
want to talk to us about?'

Then to his great surprise the giant smiled down
at him, a pleasant, good-natured smile.

'Sure, I don't want to talk to you at all,' he said,
'unless you want to talk to me. But I'd like to have
a word or two with my old friend, Beg. For I think
he could be helpful to me. He could help the wife
and myself to set right a wrong thing that we did
many years ago. It has weighed on our minds
ever since. Oh, Peter my boy,
you're young yet. But take my
advice. Never do a wrong turn
to any man. You'll live to rue
the day.'

'True for you, Meelamor,'
Edda said.

Her sharp voice suited well
with her black, bitter eyes.

'True for you.'

And to Peter she said: 'My
poor husband is losing weight
with the worry.'

The giant made a rumbling noise. In an ordinary man it might have been a sorrowful moan. But Meelamor's moan was like a roll of thunder.

Then he sighed: and his sigh, like a gale of wind, set shaking the curtains that draped the walls. The curtains behind the high chairs were tossed and parted by the wind of that sigh, and, through a wide hole in the wall, Peter saw the blue sky. In the castle of Meelamor there were no ordinary windows with glass to keep out the rain and let in the light.

'Content yourself, ma'am,' Peter said to Edda. 'It would take a great deal of worry to wear your husband to the bone.'

But Meelamor had waved his hand for silence. Looking down directly at Beg he began to speak.

He called Beg by his name. He spoke to him as a kindly man would speak to his best friend. He said: 'Beg, I need your help if you will be so kind as to give it to me.'

Then turning his huge eyes ....

They were huge, too. Each one of them was as big as a soup-plate.

Then turning his huge eyes on Peter, he told from the very beginning the sad story of King Rory. He left nothing out. Now and again he sighed and wiped his eyes with the hairy knuckles of his left hand, and each knuckle was the size of a yardbrush.

Then, when the whole story was told, he said: 'And this now is the way of it. King Rory is dead and in his grave. I can do no good to him now to make up for the evil that is done.

'But his daughter is still alive. And what's more she is here in this castle. My wish and desire is to make her the queen of the Southern Land to rule in peace over the people her father once ruled. And that's the reason, Beg, why I'm asking your help. You're the very man to tell the people of the Southern Land that the princess is the daughter of King Rory.'

'And is King Rory dead?' Beg said.

'To himself be it told,' said the giant. 'But such is indeed the case.'

'My poor master. My poor King,' Beg said.

Tear followed tear down his tiny, furrowed cheeks.

'Your sorrow touches my heart,' said Edda.

And she began to cry. Very loudly.

Then she said: 'Oh Beg, dear friend, I know you will help us to right this great wrong. You do not, you cannot feel the sorrow we feel, the way we feel it. Think what it would mean to us to pass our last days in sorrow and remorse with this great load upon our hearts. Help us. Please, help us.'

'I will indeed,' said the generous little man. 'With all my heart. With my last breath. With the last work of my hand I'll help you. Let the past be forgotten among us. Let us work all together to do good.'

At that, the giant bent down, grasped the little man in his arms, hugged him, passed him on to Edda who also hugged him and then replaced him, very dizzy and breathless, on the floor.

Then Meelamor ordered Kate to prepare a great feast and to have it ready in the evening for himself and Edda and Beg and Peter and the princess.

Peter stood listening and, with bitterness in his heart, hating Meelamor worse than ever. And when kind little Beg saw the sour look on Peter's face he said: 'What then will be the portion of my good friend, Peter, the son of Jamesy the milkman.'

Meelamor scratched his huge head. His scratching fingers made a noise like ten men digging with rusty spades in rocky ground.

'I think,' he said, 'that Peter would be well advised to go back to his father's business. After all, a good milkman is no man's mockery. And he could always marry Kate. He has my full permission.'

But just as he ceased speaking another voice spoke sharply and loudly from the far corner of the room. It was the princess. She had been there all the time although Peter and Beg had not noticed her.

'Peter will do nothing of the sort,' she cried. I want him to be a prince at my court when I am queen over the Southern Land. What do you say to that, Peter?'

Peter said nothing. Meelamor went on scratching his head. At long last he said: 'Be it so, princess. Let it be as you wish.'

But by the tone of his voice he wasn't pleased or easy in his mind.

Peter turned and looked all around the room.

Kate was no longer there to be seen. So he said to Meelamor: 'Tell me now what is to happen to Shawn the father of Kate. Where is he?'

'To Shawn, the poor and honest farmer,' Meelamor said.

'The same.'

'But the man is dead.'

'Is that so?' said Peter.

'''Tis so.'

'And what did he die of?'

'Of a plague. A black plague. That's why we didn't tell Kate. It would have been too sad.'

'You're very good and thoughtful,' said Peter.

'Ah lad,' said Meelamor, 'the longer you live, the more you learn. When you're an old man like me you'll learn to stop thinking of yourself and to start thinking about other people.'

He sighed and yawned and stretched himself and fell asleep in his chair. Edda pointed to the door and whispered to Peter and Beg that they were free to go to their room. Her whisper was like the hiss of a snake.

When they were halfway to the door she came after them. She warned them to be in good time for the great feast in the evening.

7

In the high shimmering heat of noon Peter lay down under an oak tree by the bank of the river. With lazy, half-closed eyes he watched the swift race of the water over the sandy shallows close to the shore.

And, as he lay and watched, the dark shadow of the Old One, the Trout from the Turnhole of Creevan, the King of All Trout, the Superior of the Red Salmon, the Terror of the Green Pike, came silently, as Peter had expected, from the deep places in the middle of the river.

So Peter bent down from the bank until his face almost touched the running, cool water. He waited for the magic voice:

'Peter. This is the last time in your life that you'll either see or hear me.'

'What if I hook you again on the little pointed hook?'

'That is a thing that will never come to pass,' the Old One said. 'Once hooked, twice shy. And indeed if you were everything that you should be you would leave the trout in peace to swim in the water. How would you like to be caught on a little pointed hook?'

'Now that you mention it,' said Peter. 'I wouldn't like it at all.'

'Well, there you are.'

There was an uneasy lull in the conversation.

'Still, Peter,' said the Old One, 'once upon a time you did me a good deed when I was in a sore case. And we trout flatter ourselves that our great virtue is gratitude. Now you want to find your way out of this castle and you want to marry the daughter of King Rory. This is how you'll do all that. And I have no doubt but that as you're a lad of wit and courage you'll follow my directions.'

'I'll do my level best,' Peter said. 'What more can I do?'

'Spoken like a man. Now listen carefully to me. Look out at the middle of the river. Tell me what you see there.'

'I see a small bushy island.'

'Correct,' said the trout. 'On that island there's the nest of a swan. And in that nest there are eggs. But one of those eggs is as black as black can be. And the truth is that it was never laid by a swan.'

'How then does it come to be in the nest?'

'That's a long long tale and I've little time to tell

it. Let it be enough to say that it was stolen by the
swan long before you were born. Ever since then
she has tried to hatch it. But no swan will ever come
out of that egg.'

'I can credit that,' Peter said.

'Now you must swim across and take that egg
and give it to Kate who is the daughter of Shawn.
When you crack the shell you'll find that that egg,
black as it is, is filled with a powder as white as
snow. Kate must put some of that white powder
into the cup out of which Meelamor drinks his
wine.'

'And what happens then?'

'Then,' said the Old One, 'you will see for yourself. But if I was in your shoes, I'd take a weapon with me when I go to the feast.'

'Hidden in a place, I know,' Peter said. 'I have Beg's sword.'

But the Old One was doubtful: 'Take a big stick as well. Good luck to you now. Keep a clear head, a brave heart and a steady hand. And everything will be as right as the mayfly.'

And before Peter could stand up, the Old One was gone from the sandy shallows.

But out near the middle of the river the surface of the water was broken as if some big body had passed underneath.

Widening ripples lapped against the bank. Then the current smoothed them over and everything was as it always had been.

Then and there Peter stripped and, when he had hidden his clothes in the long grass, waded out through the shallows, and out and out until the water lapped his chin. Then he kicked up his heels and started to swim.

The distance was long and the current was swift. But Peter was a strong fellow and he crossed, without any mishap, to the bushy island. He found the roughly-built nest in a clump of green reeds by the edge of the water. He found the black egg and carried it safely back to the place by the oaktree on the bank of the river. The swan was far from home gathering food and she never found out who had stolen the black egg. Which she herself had once stolen.

Then, when Peter was putting on his jacket and combing his wet hair with his fingers, he heard a light footstep coming towards him through the trees. It was the princess. Quickly he hid the black egg in a hollow at the roots of the oak tree. He stood up straight. He smiled at her as she approached. She smiled back at him.

'Was it swimming in the river, you were?' she said.

She could not help but notice his shining face and wet hair.

So, Peter said that he had been swimming in the river.

'What for?' That was her question.

'To cool myself in the heat.'

So she said that she loved to go swimming.

And he said: 'Isn't it good for you then that the river is so close to the castle.'

'It is, indeed,' said the princess.

And Peter said: 'And that the blue sea is so close to the Southern Land.'

'I'll be able to go swimming often when I'm the Queen.'

That was what she said.

'Be careful then,' said Peter. 'Be careful that you don't drown. Good queens are scarce.'

'Don't you know that I will be a good queen?'

'Oh, you might at that,' said Peter. 'It's hard to tell.'

She sat down on the soft deep grass. She began to break into little pieces a fallen twig, and to throw the pieces, one by one, into the water. He sat down beside her. He picked up another twig and broke it into three pieces. He threw them into the air together and caught them in his left hand as they were coming down. He was always very clever with his hands.

She said: 'Were you surprised when I stood up for you before Meelamor?'

'No more than Meelamor was himself, by all appearances. Besides, the daughter of King Rory is free to command my services when and where she pleases.'

'You are very good,' said the princess. 'Did you wonder why I did it?'

'Did what?'

'Asked Meelamor to allow you to live in the Southern Land when I'd be queen.'

'I don't wonder,' said Peter. 'Your reasons are your own.'

The princess frowned a little. She might have

been expecting another and a more civil answer.

She said: 'I want you at the Court, Peter, because when I'm the queen I want you to be the king.'

'Well now,' said Peter, 'that's what my poor father would call putting things plainly. No doubt at all about it, the plan you mention has many good points. But do you not think that there would be more wisdom in less haste when you're choosing a husband for yourself and a ruler for your people?'

'I know my own business best,' the princess said.

Her voice was high and hard and haughty.

'I see no reason why you shouldn't make a good king. As for ruling the people, Meelamor can look after that and leave us in peace.'

'I see now,' said Peter. 'Meelamor would still have his big finger in the pie. I wonder what the people would say to all this.'

'Let them say what they please. They won't have the power to annoy us.'

'No,' said Peter. 'I could take my bible oath you wouldn't worry your pretty head about the people, or about what the people would think or say. And, sure enough, I see no good reason why I shouldn't be a king. Especially since you're good enough to offer me the job.'

So he slipped his arm around her waist and embraced her. And at that very moment Kate walked out from under the trees. She stood close to them. Her eyes were burning with a light that was half anger and half wounded affection.

'What could *you* want?' the princess said.

'Nothing from *you*,' said Kate. 'But Meelamor wants to speak to you.'

'Then I must leave you for a little, Peter my love,' said the princess.

Lightly she touched his cheek with her soft, perfumed hand. Then she ran away under the trees towards the castle.

Kate didn't even look at Peter. She turned her back on him and walked away. She planted her feet very firmly on the ground. But her shoulders were heaving and her face was pale, and the bitter tears were not very far from her eyes.

Peter stepped forward as if he were going to follow her. Then he changed his mind and sat down again under the oak tree. In his right hand he held the large key and the small key that he had unhooked from the girdle of the princess when he put his arm around her waist.

Peter was always very clever with his hands.

He might not have been too clever in other ways. But he could take a hint. He could put two and two together, and Meelamor and Edda and the princess were now in conference and very soon the princess would notice that the keys were missing, and there was no time to waste.

In less than five minutes he was tiptoeing, quietly and unnoticed, across the steaming kitchen. He opened the door with one of the stolen keys. He let himself into the cobwebbed tunnel. He locked the door again behind him to prevent anyone following him.

In the niche in the wall he found the candle and the flint. With the lighted candle in one hand and in the other hand the two keys, he went on his downward way to the door of the dungeon. He found it and slipped the key into the lock and, as the door opened, he saw, by the yellow light of the candle, Shawn, the father of Kate, sitting on a low stool, his head resting sorrowfully on his hands.

Without saying a word Peter placed his hand on that grey head and made slowly the sign of the cross.

8

In the same huge room in which Meelamor and Edda had sat on high chairs to speak to Beg and Peter, the table was prepared for the feast.

Meelamor and Edda sat side by side at the head of the table. To the right hand of Meelamor sat the princess and facing her across the table was little Beg on a very high chair. Peter sat beside Beg.

The work of fetching and carrying was left to Kate. It wasn't light work, for Meelamor's appetite suited his size. But as she came and went around the table Beg looked at her and thought that she had, all of a sudden, grown as beautiful as the princess: even though Kate was dressed in rags and tatters and the proud princess wore the loveliest clothes ever woven on a loom.

That sudden beauty puzzled the little man for a while. But he wasn't a great thinker nor a good man at solving puzzles. So he gave the matter up and went on talking and eating.

Most of the talking was done by Beg and

Meelamor. Edda and the princess were dark, silent women by nature. And Peter was too busy watching Meelamor to find time to say anything.

But the giant talked enough to keep half a dozen feasts in conversation. Mostly he talked about the glory that would come to the Southern Land when the daughter of King Rory would sit on the throne. He said again and again that he was so happy to be able to restore the princess to her rightful place.

The more he talked the more he drank. The more he drank the more he talked: until in the end his big, thick tongue was flailing about in his mouth, and his face was flushed and his eyes were gleaming with the power of the wine. And his voice like continuous thunder was booming in the rafters.

And all this time Peter had hidden under the table, and settled securely under his feet, not the little shining sword of little Beg, but a big, thick blackthorn stick. As the Old One had advised him to do.

Now how did he get the big blackthorn stick in there?

He had his feet very firmly on it, in case it would move or rattle.

This was how.

He had cut it from a blackthorn bush beside the river when he reclaimed the black egg from the hole at the roots of the oak tree, and when he tossed the two keys on the ground just as if the princess had dropped them there by accident.

But, I mean, how did he get the big blackthorn stick in under the table? I mean, how could you, or me or Peter or anybody else, go into a banquet carrying a big blackthorn stick?

Now I myself have a big blackthorn stick that's all of five feet long. You could flatten ten giants with it.

But that's another story about that big blackthorn stick, and about how a man who can sing six hundred songs cut it for me from a bush in a gully in a glen in Donegal, and if you write me a letter I'll tell you the story of the man and the stick and the six hundred songs.

But come back to Peter and the blackthorn under the table.

You have guessed. I know you have guessed.

Peter had given the big blackthorn to Kate before the banquet began. That was when he had told her about the big key and the little key, and about the black egg and the white powder, and about her father, and about everything the Old One had told him, and which I haven't told you yet.

But hold on now. You'll work it out for yourselves.

~

The banquet went on and on. They drank toasts to this and to that and to everything in between.

Do you know what toasts are?

No, not the burnt bits of bread that pop up in the morning on the rack. But everyone has a glass of wine in his hand or her hand, and the gentlemen stand up and the ladies stay sitting, and the toastmaster or the master of ceremonies says Here's a Health to Somebody or Other, and everybody drinks, and glasses clink, until their own health is no better than it might be.

Because of the stick Peter had to be extra careful when he stood up. You see it might rattle and reveal itself. Or roll away under the big table to where he couldn't reach it.

And again and again they drank toasts.

Clink glasses, clink, talk and laugh, nod and wink with them.

A poet who was a friend of mine wrote that last bit as part of a song.

Toasts to Meelamor and to Edda and to the princess, and even to Beg and to Peter, and to the memory of King Rory and to the future good fortune of his daughter on her throne in the Southern Land.

No toasts, not even one, to Kate who was doing all the work and who now seemed to be, even to the eyes of Peter, as beautiful as

Cleopatra or the Queen of Sheba.

Then Meelamor called for one last toast. This one was to be to the princess, to wish her a long life and a contented rule over her father's people.

Kate filled a tall, golden drinking-cup. She filled it with wine as red as your blood or mine. With some effort, because it was as big as a bucket and very heavy, she lifted up the golden drinking-cup and placed it on the table before Meelamor. To do all that she had to walk up a bit of a ladder to get to the table and then stand on two chairs. But she did it. She was a very nimble girl and very quick on her feet.

She placed the drinking-cup down before Meelamor who was as stupid as he was big. But before she did so she passed her right hand around the shining brim of the drinking-cup. That was the secret sign that Peter had told her to make.

He kept his feet steady on the black stick.

Because in that cup was the white powder out of the black egg out of the swan's nest on the little bushy island in the middle of the river that flowed partly underneath and partly beside the castle of Meelamor.

Edda drank to the toast. The princess drank, or sipped, to her own health and her future happiness and prosperity. Meelamor drank with a gulp, or with three gulps: for poor Kate had to run here and there, and climb up and down, and fill the big drinking-cup two more times. Oh, Meelamor was a glutton and he belched like thunder.

Beg drank a little out of his own small cup. But Peter did not drink, and when Meelamor saw that, a frown of anger darkened his drunken face.

He shouted at Peter: 'You haven't tasted your wine.'

'No,' said Peter, 'I have drunk enough wine for one night.'

He spoke slowly and clearly. Under the table and most carefully he drew the blackthorn towards him with his left foot. His heart, though, was beating like a shoemaker's hammer. What on earth, or on anywhere else, would he or could he do if the slippery Old One had told him lies?

'You'll drink this toast,' roared Meelamor.

Then suddenly he shivered a giant of a shiver.

Peter watched him closely. For a moment of time the powder seemed to have no effect. Then a bewildering thing began to happen. Even Beg noticed it, and he opened his little mouth, as wide as it could open, with the force of shock and amazement.

Because Meelamor was swiftly shrinking. He was becoming smaller and smaller.

Edda's face went white with fear. The princess screamed. Beg hopped down from his chair to the floor. But Meelamor couldn't see himself as they could see him. So he just became more and more angry with Peter. In drunken rage he flung his wine cup along the table. Since the table was high where he was and lower where the others were, the cup rolled and rattled on until it banged and rang against the far wall of the room.

Again he roared at Peter: 'You'll drink this toast.'

But it wasn't much of a roar. Like himself his roar was shrinking.

So Peter, who was feeling a bit better, said that he would not drink the toast. And he said to Meelamor that he would tell the shrinking giant the reason why he, Peter, would not drink that toast. He said, and he said it out grand and loud:

'Your day is done, Meelamor. And the day of your wife Edda. And the day of your proud daughter who sits there pretending to be the daughter of a king. King Rory is free from the dungeon where you locked him in. He's free of the wicked spells your wife laid on him. And the daughter of King Rory is Kate. And you forced her to work as a servant in your castle.'

That was the longest speech Peter had ever made. He was breathless when he got to the end of it. But not so breathless that he couldn't jump up from his chair, grab the big blackthorn and take a run at Meelamor.

Edda and the princess screamed. Edda tried to rush out of the room to find her book of spells. But Kate had locked the door. And Edda knew no spell to open locked doors. Beg fell over himself with surprise and Kate pulled him out of the way of the tramping feet.

Meelamor wobbled when he stood up. Was it the weakness or was it the wine, or both? But he raised two fists that were still as big as footballs and made as if he would hammer Peter into the floor. So Peter altered course and jumped up onto and ran along the table, and thumped Meelamor twice on the back of the head. Gold and glass and silver went crashing to the floor as Meelamor turned and pounded at Peter, and missed and pounded the table. Edda and her daughter were screaming like seagulls but there was nothing they could do to halt the nimble leaps of Peter nor the thumps of the blackthorn. Then the knuckles of Meelamor's right hand began to bleed, and he looked at them and licked them, and, for the first time, it dawned on him that something had gone wrong and was rapidly getting worse.

He could see that his fist was shrinking. Worse still he didn't seem to have the strength to raise it for another blow.

Yet with the desperation of fear in his red eyes, which were now only the size of saucers, he rushed at Peter, and tripped one foot over the other and went head-over-heels over the table and got the blackthorn, six times in a row and in a hurry, on the crown of his head.

He got up and ran like a rabbit. Just at that moment a loud knock thundered on the door. Kate rushed to it, pulled the key out of her pocket and turned the lock. And into the room stepped Shawn, the father of Kate, or King Rory, as you all must now learn to call him, with his memory all restored to him, and the smile of victory on his lips, and the other big blackthorn, that Peter had also cut, in his right hand.

For one moment Meelamor hesitated. But Peter, with new strength and courage, rushed to the attack and Meelamor went on running. Down the length of the room he went with Peter hot on his heels: past the empty high chairs where he and Edda had sat to receive Beg and Peter, straight for the waving, black curtains that covered the wall and the wide opening through which air, too much of it, came into the room.

When Peter reached that spot and looked down the dizzy heights of the castle wall, Meelamor was still falling. He struck the river close to the bushy island. There was a white flash of upflung water. Then the river flowed on as black and smooth as it had ever been.

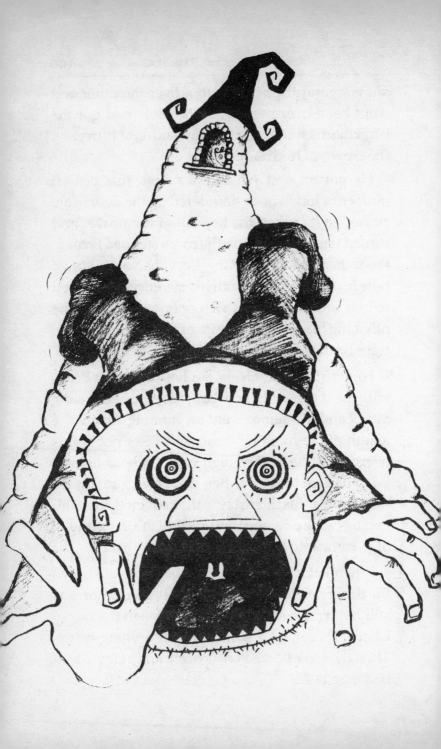

~

I suppose there's no need for me to tell you how Peter married Kate, the real princess.

They lived to rule the Southern Land after the death of King Rory at the age of ninety-nine, and they were loved by their people.

They had seven sons and seven daughters and Beg was godfather to two of the sons and two of the daughters.

Jamesy and Mary, the father and mother of Peter, went to live in the Southern Land. Jamesy became official milkman to His Majesty the King.

The rich men who were too lazy to milk their own cows grumbled, of course, when they lost the services of Jamesy and Peter. But you'll find out that it isn't possible to please everybody, not even at the end of a story.

The rich men were compelled to milk their own cows. But the hard work made many of them healthy and honest; and some of them even gave away their riches and died poor, and saved their souls into the bargain.

As for Edda and her daughter, people say they were pardoned by King Rory, even if he did make Edda burn her book of spells. The two of them went on living in the castle of Meelamor until one windy night the towers were blown down on top of them. They were never seen or heard of again.

Be that as it may!

When I passed that way some time ago there was a great heap of stones close to the bank of the river. That was all that was left of the castle of Meelamor.

And out in the water and near the bushy island there was a high pillar of stone. That was all that was left of Meelamor. For they say that the water acting on the white powder out of the black egg out of the swan's nest changed him to stone.

And there he is to this day, with the river flowing past. A warning to all wicked giants.

I see no reason to doubt any of these things.

Particularly since the Trout in the Turnhole of Creevan ....

But there, I promised him that his name would not appear in this story any more than was necessary. On that account I am not even at liberty to tell you how I made his acquaintance.

For if I did so I fear that many a fisherman of the trout would be green with envy. As green as the grass in Creevan meadow.

BOOKS WITH A BITE FROM
WOLFHOUND PRESS

CINDERELLA'S FELLA

A first book by fourteen-year-old
Aislinn O'Loughlin

You're a Prince named Fred, but dad the King calls you 'Charming'. Now he wants you to hold a ball. And find yourself a wife. Things just can't get any worse. Or can they?

Enter wobbly Priscilla and screeching Rosemary. And exit the best-looking girl at the ball — in a midnight disappearing act. But help is at hand as Prince Fred's sisters and friends come to the rescue (backwards on a horse!).

The surprising and hilarious story of Cinderella — from a guy who was really there.

'There is nothing I do not like about this story. It is very funny and exciting.'

Niamh Murphy age 11
0 86327 493 5

THE MAGIC SWORD:
A Badger, Beano adventure

Jack Scoltock

This is the third book starring Badger and Beano. Badger's father has been snatched by Curselees and taken to the Underworld. Without magic Badger must rescue him in another fast-paced, action-packed adventure with a host of weird and wonderful characters.

Badger, Beano and the Magic Mushroom
'A roller-coaster of a ride through the fantastic.'
RTE Guide
ISBN 0 86327 513 3

THE SHOP THAT NEVER SHUTS

Martin Waddell

'McGlone was the leader of the Gang because she was the biggest, and the one who had the most ideas.'

McGlone lives at the Shop that Never Shuts, and Flash and Buster Cook are in McGlone's Gang with wee Biddy O'Hare.

In these five highly entertaining stories the Gang dig for Viking treasure, are frightened that a seamonster has eaten Biddy, discover that McGlone needs glasses, look after the Shop that Never Shuts on their own, and give Biddy a birthday party.

'Exceedingly funny.'

Bookquest
ISBN 0 86327 511 7